The Zoo
at
Night

The Zoo at Night

by

Martha Robinson

illustrated by

Antonio Frasconi

Margaret K. McElderry Books

In memory of my father
Robert Bigger Stewart
— M.R.

To Luisa
— A.F.

Text copyright © 1995 by Martha Robinson
Illustrations copyright © 1995 by Antonio Frasconi
Margaret K. McElderry Books
An imprint of Simon & Schuster Children's Publishing Division
1230 Avenue of the Americas
New York, New York 10020
The text of this book is set in Grouch BT.
The illustrations are mixed-media woodcuts.
First edition
Printed in Singapore on recycled paper
10 9 8 7 6 5 4 3 2 1
Library of Congress Cataloging-in-Publication Data
Robinson, Martha.
The zoo at night / Martha Robinson ; illustrated by Antonio Frasconi.
p.   cm.
Summary: Describes what happens at the zoo when night falls and all the people leave.
ISBN 0-689-50608-2
[1. Zoos—Fiction.   2. Animals—Fiction.   3. Night—Fiction.   4. Stories in rhyme.]   I. Frasconi, Antonio, ill.   II. Title.
PZ8.3.R585Zo   1995
[E]—dc20   94-12773

What happens when they close the zoo
And all the people go away?
Do animals lie down and sleep
From sunset until dawn next day?

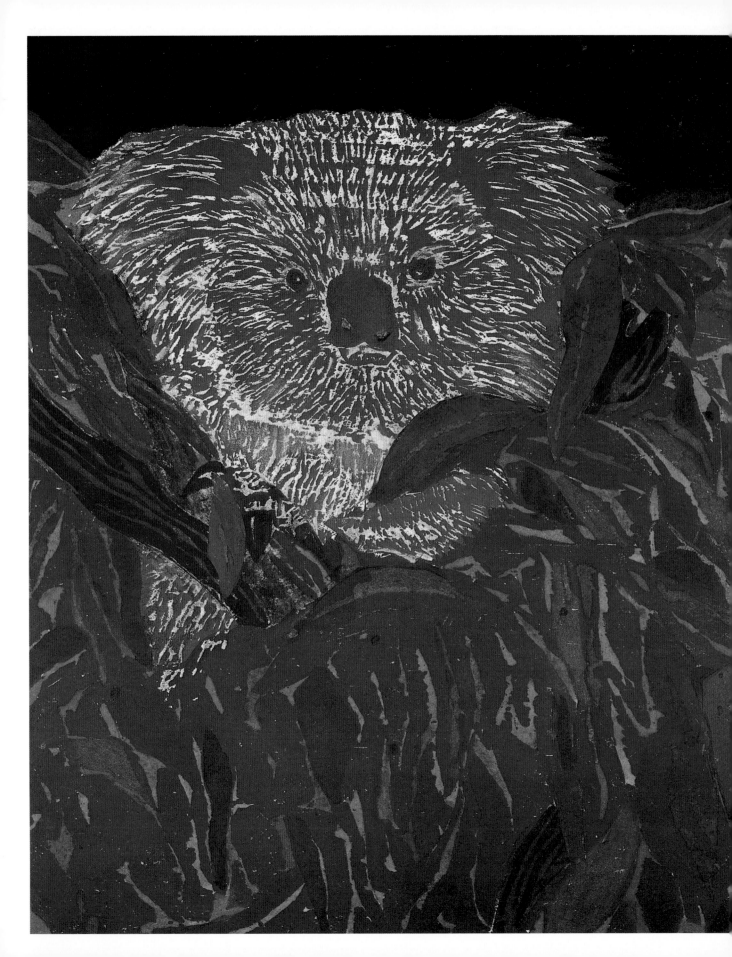

Koala munches juicy leaves
In his eucalyptus tree.
He hears the lonely far-off sound
Of coyotes howling hungrily.

From the bushes patter, rustle,
And a strange, wild cry.
Peacocks flying to their roost
Are screeching, rushing by.

A wrinkled forehead, little eyes
Float on the sunset-colored pond.
Could this be hippopotamus?
Oh, yes, it could. It is. He yawned!

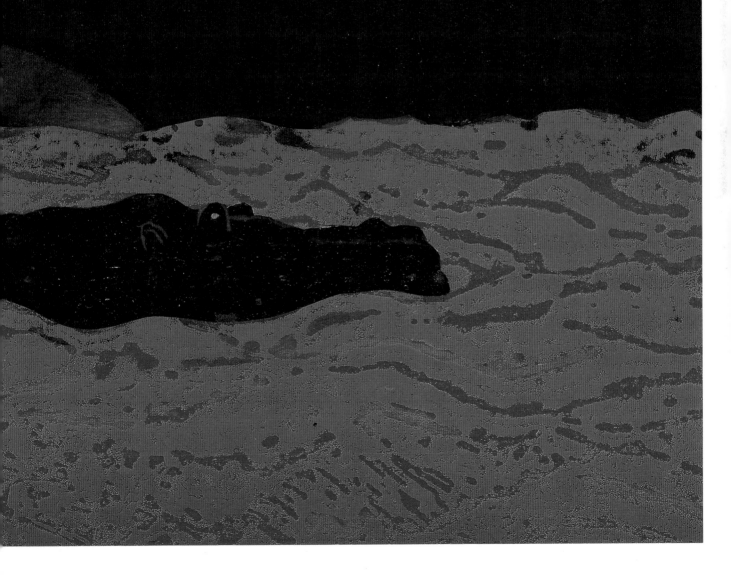

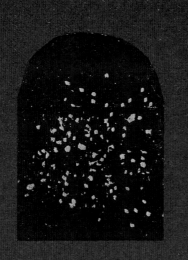

In their house the elephants
Close together stand,
Murmuring the secrets
Only they can understand.

Majestic eagle rests her head
Upon her mighty folded wing
And falls asleep as cosily
As any little feathered thing.

Busy, wide-awake raccoons
Chitter-chatter to each other.
Sleepy tiger cubs are cuddling
Closer to their mother.

Big as a couch, rhinoceros
Snuffles, sleeping on the ground.
Tiny tree frogs have begun
Their constant croaking nighttime sound.

The giant tortoise turns his head,
Looks and sees that all is well
Before he settles down to rest
In the comfort of his shell.

Alligator slowly climbs
From his lake and lies
Still as a stick, the rising moon
Reflected in his eyes.

Spider monkey dozes, wakes,
Leaps up and starts to play,
Swinging on his ropes and bars
As if the night were day.

Polar bears lie sleeping in
The coolest corner they can find.
One dreamily lifts up his head
To sniff the summer wind.

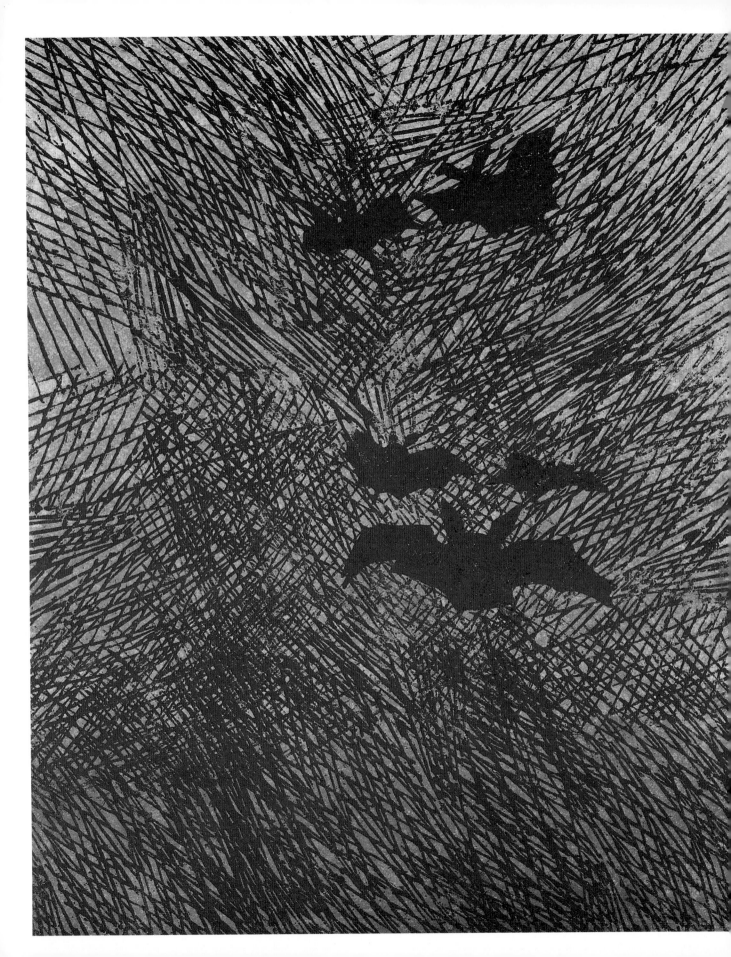

In the shadows jaguar stirs.
He glares with a glittering eye.
Fruit bats feed and stretch their wings
And lazily they fly.

Wombat sits beneath his tree
Like a creature carved in stone.
Tomorrow—sleep, but now he keeps
Watch through dark of night alone.

The moon hangs high among the stars.
All the zoo is still.

Outside the gates a coyote howls,
And lopes across the hill.